Sofia the Snail

The little snail that was afraid of the dark.

© 2013, Danielle R. Lindner
CreateSpace Publishing Company

ISBN-13: 978-1484917466
ISBN-10: 1484917464

I won't go to sleep in that scary dark shell
Every night to her mother
Sofia would yell

It's dark and it's cold
It's really too small

Every night it was something
Too big or too tight

Too hot or too cold
Too dark or too light

The shell is too brown
It's too hard it's too tough

It's too smooth
It's too rough

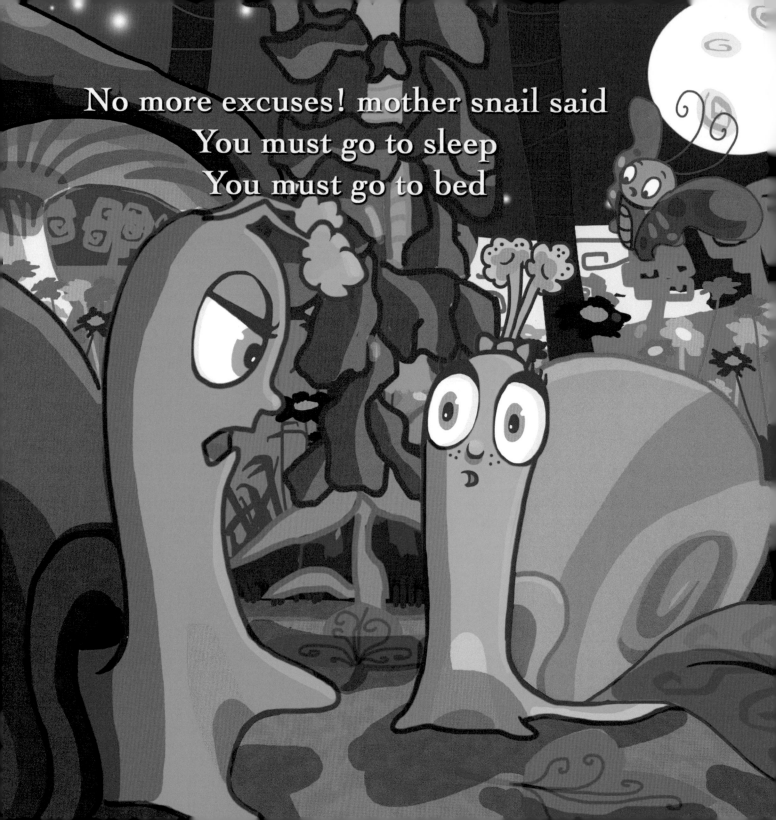

No more excuses! mother snail said
You must go to sleep
You must go to bed

And she tugged at Sofia
But she'd cry and she'd pout

I won't go inside there, Sofia would shout!

Why won't you sleep in your shell? Mother said

Close up your eyes and just lay down your head

But Sofia just sat there
Oh Mother, I'll die!

If you put me in there I'll be eaten alive

Whenever I'm sleeping I have a great fright
I see scary monsters
They come out at night

They jump out of my closet
They sit on my bed

Whenever I'm in there and wake up at night
My shell becomes haunted
Till I turn on my light

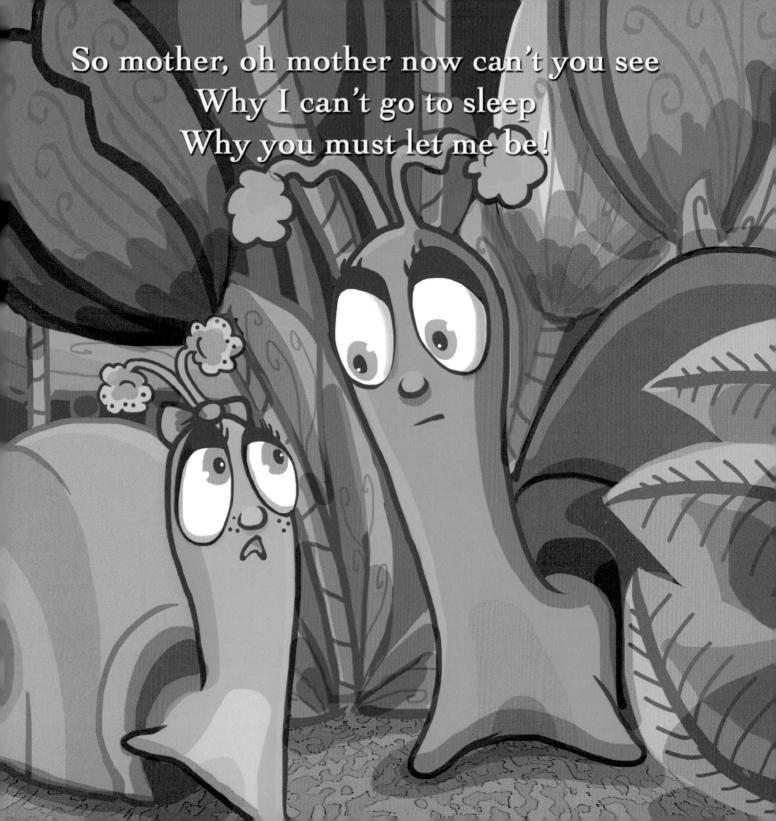

So mother, oh mother now can't you see
Why I can't go to sleep
Why you must let me be!

I'll stay with you a while
I'll turn out the light

See there are no monsters
Not one in sight

Look in the closet
Look under the bed

There are no monsters
With horns on their head

Sofia was frightened and was covering her eyes
But soon put her hands down
And found a surprise

Her eyes had adjusted
And Sofia could see
All of her bedroom
As clear as could be

The light was not on
But her room was the same

You must have scared them
She said to her mother
You are the best, a mom like no other

Sofia, Sofia
It was all in your head
Only the shadows danced on your bed

The darkness is friendly
It means it is night
Time to be sleeping
To be tucked in tight

To have wonderful dreams
Of what you love best
To give you some time
To catch up on your rest

The moon and the stars
Come out and play too
To make silly shadows
And watch over you

So sleep tight in your shell
And do not feel fright
Have wonderful dreams

And a very good night

zzzzzzz

About the Author

Danielle Lindner, a member of the SCBWI (Society for Children's Book Writers & Illustrators), has a BA in Political Science and a Master of Arts in Teaching from Fairleigh Dickinson University. She is the Founder of The London Day School® Preschool and Kindergarten Enrichment Academies.

The London Day School® was created by Ms. Lindner who saw a need for an enriching, challenging and socially engaging program for young children. Her schools and books provide a scaffolding approach to learning with a strong focus on character education.

Her books help children find their voice and become caring, nurturing and self-confident individuals. Sofia the Snail, "The little snail that was afraid of the dark." is the first book in a series of character education stories for young children that she has written.

Ms. Lindner is also a contributor to The Alternative Press as the author of Nursery U, articles for parents and educators. She is the mother of two children and actively participates in community projects and programs that support and foster the wellness and joy of children.

Acknowledgements

I would like to thank my husband & my two beautiful girls who inspire me to write & are always willing to listen to rewrite after rewrite. I would also like to thank my parents for their encouragement & support and the wonderful students and staff of The London Day School who provide so much inspiration for my books. Thank you to Deanna for her support and encouragement during my writing process & of course a big thank you to Justo Borrero who's gorgeous illustrations bring my characters to life.

Made in the USA
Columbia, SC
11 January 2019